Going Batty

by ABBY KLEIN

illustrated by
JOHN McKINLEY

Scholastic Inc.
New York Toronto London Auckland
Sydney Mexico City New Delhi Hong Kong

To my favorite bat—Amy Badt, the best
kindergarten teacher in the world!

Lots of love,
—A.K.

ISBN 978-0-545-13047-9

Text copyright © 2010 by Abby Klein
Illustrations copyright © 2010 by John McKinley
All rights reserved. Published by Scholastic Inc.
SCHOLASTIC, LITTLE APPLE, and associated logos are trademarks
and/or registered trademarks of Scholastic Inc.

12 11 10 9 8 7 6 5 4 3 2 1   10 11 12 13 14 15/0

Printed in the U.S.A.   40
First printing, July 2010

CHAPTERS

I have a problem.

A really, really big problem.

I can't sleep at night, because I keep

hearing these strange noises in my

attic. I don't know what is making

them, but they're really scary.

Let me tell you about it.

CHAPTER 1

Wake Up, Sleepyhead

Brrrrriiiinnnnng . . . brrrrriiiinnnnng! My alarm clock rang loudly in my ear.

"It can't be morning already," I said, opening one eye. "I just fell asleep."

I rolled over to grab the alarm clock and turn it off, but I fell out of bed and hit the floor with a thud. "Umph!"

Brrrriiiinnng . . . brrrrriiiiinnnnng . . . brrrriiiiinnnnng! The alarm kept ringing.

"Hey, Shark Breath, turn that thing off!" my sister, Suzie, yelled from the other room.

I got up on my hands and knees, grabbed the clock, and threw it across the room. It bounced off my dresser and crashed to the floor. The back of it opened up and the batteries fell out, but at least it stopped ringing.

"Finally!" Suzie yelled.

I lay down on the floor and closed my eyes. I was so tired I didn't think I could climb back into my bed.

Just then my mom opened my door and ran in. "What's going on in here, Freddy? I was downstairs making breakfast, and I heard a loud crash in your room."

She looked around, but she didn't see me lying on the floor. "Freddy? Freddy? Where are you?"

"I'm down here, Mom," I said. "On the floor next to my bed."

"Oh my goodness, Freddy! Are you all right?" my mom said as she rushed over to me.

"I'm fine, Mom."

"Are you hurt? Is your arm broken?"

"Freddy's arm is broken?" Suzie asked, running into the room with her toothbrush in her hand. "Let me see."

"My arm is not broken!" I yelled.

"You don't have to yell," Suzie said. "What are you doing on the floor, then, Ding-Dong?"

"Here. Let me help you up," said my mom, reaching out her hand.

She pulled me up, and we sat down on the bed together. "Now, why in the world were you sleeping on the floor?"

"I wasn't sleeping on the floor. I fell out of bed when my alarm went off."

"But I also heard a crash," said my mom. "Like something broke."

"That would be the alarm clock," Suzie said, pointing to the pieces of broken clock on my floor.

"Freddy, what happened to the clock?" asked my mom.

"I'll tell you what happened to it," said Suzie. "Freddy threw it across the room. It hit his dresser and broke into a bunch of pieces."

"Thanks a lot," I whispered to Suzie.

"You're welcome," she whispered back with a big smile on her face.

"Freddy," said my mom, "why would you throw your clock across the room?"

"Because I just wanted it to stop ringing so I could go back to sleep," I said with a big yawn.

"But it's a school day," said my mom. "You have to get up and go to school."

"Do I have to?" I said, yawning again. I lay back down on the bed.

"That is so not fair!" said Suzie. "I never get to stay home just because I'm tired." Toothpaste started dripping out of her mouth.

"Who said anything about staying home?" said my mom. "And I think you need to go rinse out your mouth before any of that toothpaste drips on the carpet."

Suzie put her hand up to her mouth to catch the dripping toothpaste and ran off to the bathroom.

As soon as Suzie left, my dad walked into the room. "Is everything all right up here? Your mom came to check on you, but she never came back down. I was starting to get worried."

"Everything is fine, Daniel," said my mom.

"Then why isn't Freddy getting dressed and ready for school?"

I pulled the covers over my head. "I'm too tired to go to school!"

"Too tired?" said my dad.

"Too tired?" said my mom. "But, Freddy, why are you so tired? You went to bed early last night."

"I know," I said from under the covers, "but

I keep hearing these strange noises, and I can't sleep."

"Oh no! Not this again," my dad said. "I thought we took care of the vampire nightmares with the Dream Police."

"It's not a vampire, Dad," I said. "I think it's a monster."

"A monster," Suzie said, laughing.

"Go away!" I yelled. "No one invited you back into the room."

"But I just have to hear about this monster," Suzie said, giggling. "Does he live under your bed or in your closet?"

"For your information, he doesn't live in either of those places, Brat. He lives in the attic."

"The attic?" Suzie said. "That's a good one, Freddy."

"The attic?" asked my dad. "There is nothing in that attic except a lot of old junk."

"I don't think there is anything up there that a monster would like," said my mom.

"Besides," said my dad, "the Dream Police will take care of the monster if there is one. They can get rid of any nightmare."

"But it's not a nightmare. It's a real monster," I said. "And the Dream Police can't get up to the attic."

"I'll tell you what," said my dad, pulling the covers off my head. "We can talk about this more later, but right now you need to get up, get dressed, and get ready for school."

"Let's go, Sleepyhead," said my mom. "I don't want you to miss the bus."

"Can't I just stay home and sleep? Pleee-eeease."

"No!" said Suzie.

I stuck my tongue out at her. "Who asked you?" I said.

"Enough, you two," said my dad. "You both

need to get moving or you're going to be late. Hop to it!"

My dad lifted me out of bed and carried me into the bathroom. "Splash some water on your face. That should wake you up. I want to see you downstairs in five minutes. You will be in big trouble if you miss your bus."

"Yes, Dad," I mumbled.

CHAPTER 2

Who's Afraid of Monsters?

I ran out my front door just as the bus pulled up. "Whew, that was lucky," I thought.

I dragged myself up the steps of the bus, walked slowly up the aisle, and sat down next to my best friend, Robbie.

"Are you okay?" Robbie asked. "You look terrible."

"Gee, thanks," I said. "I'm fine. I just didn't get enough sleep last night."

"But I thought you said your mom wasn't

going to let you stay up to watch that shark program on TV."

"She didn't."

"Then why are you so tired?"

"Monsters."

"Monsters?" said Robbie.

"Yeah, monsters," I said.

Just then Chloe turned around in her seat

and said, "Would you two please stop talking about monsters? You're scaring me."

"You're such a baby," said Max, the biggest bully in the whole first grade. "Monsters are cool!"

"No, they are not!" said Chloe. "And besides, my nana told me there is no such thing as monsters."

"My *abuela*, my grandma, told me the same thing," said my friend Jessie.

"Well, guess what?" I said. "They are real, and one of them is living in my attic!"

"That's a good one, Freddy," said Robbie, laughing.

"I'm not kidding," I said. "There really is a monster up in my attic."

"No, there isn't," said Robbie.

"Yes, there is," I said.

"What does he look like?" asked Max. "Does he have three eyes and horns on his head?"

"Stop it! Stop it right now!" Chloe said, covering her ears. "You are scaring me! I'm going to tell on you!"

"Have you ever seen him?" asked Jessie.

"No," I said.

"Then how do you know he's there?" asked Robbie.

"He makes all these weird noises," I said.

"Cool!" said Max. "Like what?"

"Stop it! Stop it!" Chloe yelled again.

"Be quiet, you little princess," said Max. "Why don't you just go sit in another seat?"

"I think I will. Then I won't have to be near you, Mr. Stinky Max Sellars," Chloe said, and she stuck out her tongue at Max.

Max started laughing and pointing at Chloe. "You look like a frog!" he said. "Actually, a big, ugly, wet toad!"

"Wahhhhh!" Chloe wailed. She picked up her frilly pink princess backpack and moved to a seat near the front of the bus.

"Now that she's gone," said Max, "tell me what kind of noises it makes."

"Well," I said, "sometimes I hear this scratching sound, like this: SCRRRRAAATCH . . . SCRRRRAAATCH."

"Then he must have claws. Really big claws."

"Maybe," I said.

"Yeah," said Max, "and he's scratching on the attic door because he wants to come out."

I felt a shiver run down my back, but I didn't want Max to think I was scared.

"Did you ever notice any scratch marks on your attic door?" asked Jessie.

"No," I said. "But I think the monster just started living in my attic a few days ago."

"What other kinds of noises do you hear?" asked Max.

"Kind of like a screaming, squeaking sound," I said, "like this: EEEEEEEEEK . . . EEEEEEEEEEK."

"You probably just have mice running around

in the attic," said Robbie. "They can scratch and squeak."

"I think I know what a mouse sounds like," I said. "I'm not dumb."

"Do you hear any other noises?" asked Jessie.

"Sometimes I hear a weird thumping."

"Wow! Really?" said Max. "He must be really huge. That thumping must be him walking around on his big feet."

Now I was starting to get really scared.

"Did you go up to your attic to check it out?" asked Max.

"Uh . . . no," I said.

"Why not?"

"Because . . . because . . . ummm . . . because."

"Because I bet you're too scared," said Max. "That's it. Baby Freddy is too scared."

"I am not!" I lied.

"Oh, yes, you are!" said Max. "You are a little

chicken." Max started to flap his arms and make
clucking sounds. "Cluck, cluck, cluck."

"No, he's not," said Jessie. Jessie was the only
one brave enough to stand up to Max.

"Then why can't he tell us what the monster
looks like?" said Max.

"Because Freddy just hasn't had time to check it out yet. Right, Freddy?" asked Jessie.

"Yeah . . . right," I said. I couldn't tell Max that I hadn't checked it out because I *was* too scared. He would call me a baby for the rest of my life!

"Well then, Freddy can check it out this weekend and tell us all about it next week," said Max.

I gulped. "Yeah. Sure thing," I said. Max would never know if I actually went up to the attic. I could just pretend that I did. I could just make up a story next week about what the monster looked like.

"And no pretending," said Max. "I want to see a picture of this thing, so you'd better take your camera with you."

Oh boy. Now I was really in trouble. There was no way I was ever going to stay in that attic long enough to take a picture of a monster. I would have to tell Max the truth, that I was just a big fraidy-cat. But before I could say anything, Jessie answered for me.

"No problem," said Jessie. "If there is a monster in his attic, then Freddy will have that picture for you next week. Right, Freddy?"

I gulped again. "Yeah . . . right."

CHAPTER 3

Going Batty

I was glad that bus ride was finally over. All that talk of monsters was really scaring me.

I walked slowly to class.

"What are you going to do now?" asked Robbie.

"I don't know," I moaned. "I think I'm in big trouble!"

"Well, maybe I can help you," said Robbie.

"You can?" I said.

"I just have to get my mom to let me sleep

over at your house, and then we can go monster hunting together," said Robbie.

"That would be awesome!" I said. "You're the best friend ever!"

We had reached the classroom, so we went in, put away our stuff, and sat down on the rug.

"Good morning, boys and girls," said our teacher, Mrs. Wushy. "Since Halloween is coming up, I thought it would be fun if we learned about some spooky creatures."

"Like monsters?" said Max.

"Oh no . . . here we go again," I whispered to Robbie.

"No! No! No!" Chloe screamed. She put her fingers in her ears and started jumping around. "I do not want to talk about monsters."

"It's okay, Chloe. Calm down," said Mrs. Wushy. "We are not going to be talking about monsters. There is no such thing as monsters."

"Oh, yes, there is," I thought.

"How about witches?" asked Jessie.

"No, we are not going to talk about witches," said Mrs. Wushy.

"Too bad," said Chloe. "I wanted to learn how to turn Max into a donkey."

Max jumped up and started waving an imaginary wand in Chloe's direction. "I'll turn you into a lizard!" said Max.

"No, you won't!" said Chloe.

"Yes, I will!" said Max. "Abracadabra . . ."

"Stop it right now, you two," said Mrs. Wushy. "That is enough. Max, you go sit over there, and, Chloe, you sit over here. I don't want to hear another word from the two of you."

After they sat back down, Mrs. Wushy said, "I thought it would be fun if we learned about real creatures, such as bats and spiders."

"I love bats and spiders," said Robbie.

"Today we are just going to learn about bats," said Mrs. Wushy. "They are very interesting animals. Does anyone know anything about bats?"

Of course Robbie raised his hand. He is a science genius, and he knows everything about animals.

"Bats are the only mammals that fly."

"Excellent, Robbie," said Mrs. Wushy. "That is correct."

"Birds fly," said Max, "and they are animals."

"But birds are not *mammals*," said Mrs. Wushy. "Most mammals' babies are born alive. They do

not hatch from eggs. And all baby mammals
drink their mother's milk."

"I know something," said Jessie. "Bats hang
upside down. One time I saw a picture of a
whole bunch of bats hanging upside down in
a cave."

"Good," said Mrs. Wushy. "What else?"

"They live in trees or caves," I said.

"And sometimes they even live in your attic,"

said a girl named Ava. "My grandma used to have bats living in her attic."

"Does anyone know what bats eat?" asked Mrs. Wushy.

"They suck your blood," said Max. "They bite your neck with their big fangs and suck out the blood." He opened his mouth and pretended to bite the air.

"Eeewwwww! That is disgusting!" said Chloe. "I think I'm going to be sick!"

"You'd better watch out," said Max. "When Dracula leaves his castle at night, he turns into a bat. He might fly into your room and drink your blood."

"Stop it! Stop it, Max!" yelled Chloe.

I was starting to get a little freaked out myself.

"Calm down, Chloe," said Mrs. Wushy. "Dracula is not real. He is just a character in a story, and there is only one kind of bat that drinks blood. That is the vampire bat, and it does not live in the United States."

"Really?" asked Jessie. "I thought all bats drank blood."

"Most people think that," said Mrs. Wushy, "because of the Dracula story. That's why people are so afraid of bats. But they are really very gentle."

"Then what *do* they eat?" I asked.

"Most bats eat fruit or insects," said Mrs. Wushy. "The bats that live around here eat insects."

"Yuck!" said Chloe.

"I once ate an insect," said Max. "When I was little, I picked up a cricket and popped it in my mouth. It was really crunchy."

"I bet he ate more than one," Jessie whispered to me.

"Yuck, yuck, yucky, yuck!" said Chloe. "You are gross, Max."

"People don't like to eat bugs," said Robbie, "but I'm glad bats do."

"Why?" I asked.

"Because if we didn't have bats, we would have way too many insects on our planet."

"Robbie is right," said Mrs. Wushy. "If you think the mosquitoes are bad in the summer, imagine what it would be like if we didn't have bats to eat them."

"I don't think I want to imagine *that*," I said.

"Yeah," said Jessie, "I'm getting itchy just thinking about it!"

"So bats are really important to people and the planet Earth," said Mrs. Wushy. "That's why we need to take care of them and protect them."

"I know something else about bats," I said.

"Great!" said Mrs. Wushy. "What is it?"

"Bats are nocturnal."

"Who remembers what that means?" asked Mrs. Wushy.

"It means that they are awake at night and asleep in the day," said Jessie, "just like owls."

"And mice!" I said.

"That is right," said Mrs. Wushy. "And because they have to fly at night, they use something special to help them find their way in the dark."

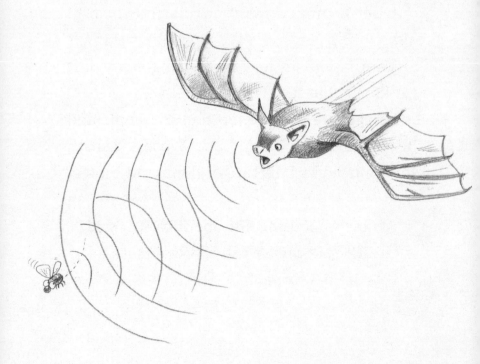

"Oh, I know! I know!" Robbie said. "They use echolocation."

"Echo . . . lo . . . what?" I said.

"Echolocation," said Robbie.

"What's that?" asked Jessie.

"A bat makes a high-pitched beeping sound. The sound waves hit an object and bounce back to the bat's ears, like an echo. The echo tells the bat the size and shape of the object and where it is located."

"Yes," said Mrs. Wushy. "It's kind of like a special way of seeing in the dark."

"I wish I had a special way of seeing in the dark," I whispered to Robbie. "Then I might be able to find that monster in my attic."

"Let's have a sleepover tonight," said Robbie. "I can't do echolocation, but I can bring my night-vision goggles. That might help us find the monster in your attic."

"Great idea!" I whispered back, but I could already feel my stomach doing flip-flops.

CHAPTER 4

Cookie Monster

As the school bus pulled up in front of my house, Robbie said, "Talk to your mom about the sleepover, and I'll talk to my mom."

"Okay," I said.

"You know you're not going to sleep until you catch that monster," said Robbie. "And you'll never do it alone, so . . ."

Just hearing Robbie say the word "monster" made a shiver run down my spine. Max must have heard us talking, because he said, "Oh yeah, Shark Boy. Remember I want a picture of that monster in your attic next week."

I looked at Max. I looked at Robbie. And then I grabbed my backpack and ran off the bus.

"Let me know what your mom says," Robbie called after me.

I ran into the house and followed a delicious smell into the kitchen. My mom and Suzie were in there making chocolate-chip cookies.

"Mmmmmmm . . . it smells yummy in here," I said.

I walked over to where my mom was mixing the batter, and stuck my finger into the bowl.

"Hey! Get your fat little fingers out of the bowl," said Suzie.

"But I love eating the batter," I said, licking my finger. I stuck my finger in again to get another taste.

"Freddy!" said my mom. "Stop sticking your dirty fingers into the bowl."

"I don't want your cooties in my cookies," Suzie said, pushing me away.

"Cookies . . . cookies . . . ," I grunted.

"What are you?" said my mom. "The Cookie Monster?"

I froze. Did she have to say that word? I had

almost forgotten about the monster in the attic.

"Go wash your hands," said my mom. "You can have some of the cookies when they come out of the oven."

I went to the sink and washed my hands.

"What are you making cookies for?" I asked.

"Actually, they're for me," said Suzie. "I'm taking them to my Girl Scout picnic tomorrow, so you really can't have too many."

"Oh, Suzie, Freddy can have some," said my mom. "We made plenty."

"Robbie and I can put ice cream in between two cookies and make homemade ice-cream sandwiches later," I said.

"You and Robbie?" asked my mom. "What do you mean?"

"I was planning on having Robbie sleep over tonight," I said.

"Since when?" said Suzie. "You never asked Mom and Dad."

"So, I'm asking Mom now," I said.

"Well, she's going to say no," said Suzie, rolling the cookie dough into balls and sticking them on the cookie sheet.

"Why is she going to say no?" I asked.

"Because you slept on the floor last night," Suzie said, putting the last few balls of dough on the tray.

"I did not. And you're not my mom," I said.

"But I am," my mom interrupted, "and I say no."

"See? What did I tell you?" Suzie said, grinning.

"Pleeeeaaase, Mom. Pretty please with a cherry on top?"

"I don't think it's a good idea," said my mom. "You haven't been sleeping well the last few nights, so you're very tired."

"You couldn't even get off the floor this morning," Suzie added.

I glared at her.

She smiled back.

"But tomorrow isn't a school day, and I think I would sleep better with a friend in the room."

"Nice try," Suzie whispered to me.

I ignored her and kept talking. "I don't think I would be as scared about the monster if I had Robbie with me."

"It's kind of late in the day to be making plans like this," said my mom.

"What?" said Suzie. "You might actually consider letting Robbie sleep over? That is so not fair!"

"I didn't say Robbie could come over," said my mom. "Calm down, Suzie."

"But you didn't say no, either. Right, Mom?" I said. "Right?"

I had to convince her to let Robbie spend the night. There was no way I was going to go monster hunting by myself. "I just know I could sleep the whole night if Robbie was in the room. The monster is not going to attack me if Robbie is there."

"Why not?" said Suzie. "He could have two juicy little boys instead of one." She smiled an evil smile.

Did she really have to say that?

"Suzie," said my mom, "don't say those kinds of things to Freddy. You're going to scare him."

"Going to . . . ," I thought. "She already has." I didn't think I was ever going to be able to sleep again, but I didn't want her to know that she had me so freaked out.

"It's okay, Mom. She doesn't scare me," I said, pretending to be brave. I felt my knees wobble.

Suddenly I heard a loud scratching sound.

"What's that?" I screamed as I jumped about three feet in the air.

"Look at you, you little fraidy-cat," Suzie said, laughing. "I just scratched my fingers on

the counter, and you jumped right out of your shoes."

"Suzie," said my mom. "That was not nice to scare your brother like that. You need to tell him you're sorry."

"But it was so funny watching him jump," said Suzie.

"Come on, Suzie. Tell Freddy you're sorry."

I glared at her.

She smiled at me.

"Suuuuuuzie," said my mom. "I'm waiting."

"Fine." Suzie turned to me. "Sorry I made you jump, you little baby."

"Suzie, just an 'I'm sorry' and nothing else," said my mom.

"Fine. I'm sorry," Suzie said.

"You can see that I am really freaked out by this whole thing, Mom," I said. "I really need someone else in the room with me tonight."

"I don't know, Freddy . . ."

Just then the phone rang.

Suzie shoved me out of the way and picked it up. "Hello?" she said. She frowned and handed me the phone. "It's for you."

I grabbed it from her.

"Hello, Freddy. It's Robbie. My mom says I can sleep over. What does your mom say?"

I turned to my mom. "Robbie's mom says he can sleep over. What do you say?"

"I don't know, Freddy . . ."

I gave her my sad puppy dog look.

"Oh, all right. I guess he can sleep over, but you have to promise me you two will *sleep*. I want you to get a good night's rest."

"I promise," I said as I crossed my fingers behind my back.

CHAPTER 5

The Plan

When Robbie's mom dropped him off, we went straight up to my room and closed the door. I didn't want Suzie to listen to us making our monster-hunting plan.

"So? What's the plan?" I said to Robbie.

"I'm still working on it," Robbie said, "but here's what I have so far. We have to wait until everyone is asleep and the house is quiet."

"That's for sure," I said. "If my mom and dad find out we're up in the attic in the middle of the night, we'll be in big trouble. I promised my mom we would be sleeping."

"So once your mom, your dad, and Suzie are asleep, we put on black shirts and black sweatpants."

"Why?"

"Because if we are dressed all in black, then we will blend in with the dark of the night, and the monster won't see us coming."

"Good thinking," I said.

"We also want to wear just socks and no shoes, because we don't want the monster to hear us climbing up the attic stairs."

"Yeah, and we have to remember to skip the fourth stair, because that one really squeaks," I said.

"We will have to bring some equipment with us," Robbie said.

"Equipment? Like what?"

"My night-vision goggles," said Robbie. "They will help us see better in the dark attic."

"What else?"

"Hockey sticks."

"Hockey sticks? Why?"

"What if the monster comes running after us? What are you going to do? We have to be able to fight."

All of a sudden this monster hunting didn't sound like such a good idea anymore.

Robbie must have seen the look on my face. "What's the matter, Freddy? Are you okay?"

"I just don't know if I can go through with this," I said.

"So you're just going to tell Max Sellars that you were too afraid to find the monster in your attic and take a picture?"

"Well . . . no . . ."

"Then you don't have a choice," said Robbie. "We have to get that picture."

"Oh no!" I said.

"What?" said Robbie.

"I forgot to get the camera."

"Where is it?" asked Robbie.

"In my parents' room."

"Well, that's the most important thing," said Robbie. "If we don't have the picture, no one will believe us."

"I know. I know," I said. I was not about to risk my life and not have proof. I had to get that camera. "You wait here. I'm going to sneak into my parents' room and grab the camera. I think it's in my mom's dresser drawer."

I quietly opened the door to my room and looked into the hall. The coast was clear. No one else was upstairs. My parents were in the kitchen and Suzie was watching TV. I tiptoed into my parents' room and slowly opened my mom's drawer. There it was! Right where I thought it would be. I grabbed the camera, shoved it into my pocket, and closed the drawer.

That was when I felt the hand on my shoulder.

Could it be . . . ? Was it . . . ? I screamed. "AAAAAHHHHHH!"

Then I heard Suzie laughing. I turned around to find her rolling on the floor, laughing her head off. "That was the funniest thing I've ever seen," she said. "You jumped so high I thought you were going to hit the ceiling."

"Oooooh . . . I'm going to get you for this," I said.

"Freddy, is everything all right up there?" my mom called from downstairs. "What is all that screaming?"

I ran to the top of the stairs. "Everything is just fine up here, Mom. We were just playing a game."

"Well, please don't scream like that. You scared me half to death."

Scared *her*? I almost had a heart attack! "Okay, Mom. I'll tell Suzie to stop screaming," I said.

Suzie turned to me. "Very funny, you little wimp. I would never scream like a baby."

"Why don't you just go back downstairs and finish watching your stupid Pretty Ponies show on TV? Robbie and I are busy."

"Busy doing what?"

"None of your beeswax," I said.

"Oh really?" said Suzie. "I know you and Robbie are up to something. You'd better tell me what it is, or else I'm going to tell Mom and Dad that you stole their camera."

"I didn't steal anything. I borrowed it."

"Did you ask Mom first?" said Suzie.

"Well, no."

"Then I'd better go tell them you have it," Suzie said as she started to head down the stairs.

"No, wait!" I said, grabbing the back of her shirt.

"Let go of me, Hammerhead," Suzie said, wiggling free from my grip. "What?"

"If I tell you, then you have to promise me that you won't tell Mom and Dad," I said.

"What's it worth to you?" said Suzie, holding up her pinkie for a pinkie swear.

"Ummm . . . ummmm . . ."

"Well? Spit it out."

"I'll clean up your room," I said.

"Deal!" Suzie said before I could take it back. "Wow! You really must not want them to know what you're up to," said Suzie.

We locked our pinkies for the pinkie swear.

"Now you have to tell me what you and Robbie are doing."

"I need that camera because I have to get a picture of the monster," I whispered.

"The monster?" said Suzie. "What monster?"

"The one in the attic," I said. "Robbie and I are going to go up there after Mom and Dad go to bed."

"You're crazy," said Suzie. "I just have one question."

"Yeah?"

"How are you going to pull down the attic stairs?"

"I haven't figured that out yet."

"Why don't you tell Dad that you need something in the attic now, so that he has to pull down the stairs?" said Suzie.

"You're a genius!" I said. "You're the best sister in the whole world!"

"I know," Suzie said, smiling.

CHAPTER 6

The Plan, Part Two

I went back into my room. "What took you so long?" asked Robbie. "And what was all that screaming about?"

"Oh, nothing . . . nothing," I said. "The good news is I got the camera." I pulled the camera out of my pocket.

"Great!" said Robbie. "Now you will have a picture to prove to Max that there really is a big, ugly monster in your attic."

I gulped. "Yeah," I said.

"Then Max won't be able to call you a baby," said Robbie. "Babies don't go monster hunting."

"Right," I said, trying to sound brave. "Babies don't go monster hunting."

I sighed. "There's only one problem with our plan."

"What's that?" said Robbie.

"The attic stairs are really heavy, so we have to think of a reason to go up there right now so my dad has to pull them down."

"Why don't you ask him if we can look at his old baseball card collection?" said Robbie.

"Good idea!" I said. "Come on!"

Robbie and I ran down the stairs.

"What's up, boys?" said my dad.

"We wanted to go up in the attic," I said.

"Now?" said my mom. "It's almost bedtime. You can go up there in the morning."

"But, Mom, we have to go now," I said.

"What do you need up there?" asked my dad.

"Robbie and I wanted to look at your old baseball card collection, Dad."

"Freddy said that you had some famous rookie cards," said Robbie. "That is so cool! I brought my collector's guide over. We wanted to see how much they're worth."

I smiled at Robbie. "Good job," I mouthed at him.

"All right," said my dad.

"But once you boys get the cards, you have to put on your pajamas and get into bed. You can look at the cards for a few minutes before you turn your light off," said my mom.

"Okay, Mom," I said.

We went back upstairs with my dad. "If you can find some of those cards in your guide, I'd love to know how much they're worth," said my dad.

"Sure thing, Mr. Thresher," said Robbie.

We walked into the guest room. That was where the attic stairs were hidden in the ceiling.

My dad gave a big tug on the string and pulled the stairs down. "Boy, these stairs are really heavy. They're also very shaky, so be careful climbing up."

We followed my dad up the attic stairs. When

we stepped on the fourth stair, it made a loud creak.

"What did I tell you?" I whispered to Robbie.

When we got up to the attic, my dad started digging through a box in the back corner. "I think this is it," he said, lifting up an old shoe box. "I'm pretty sure those cards are in here. Come on, boys. I'll carry it down."

"Can we stay up here another minute?" I asked.

"Mom said you needed to go to bed."

"Just five more minutes," I said. "There is something I really want to find to show Robbie."

"Five minutes. I'll put this box of my old cards in your room. Then I'm going to go tell your mom I found the old quilt she was looking for. I'll be right back." My dad disappeared down the stairs.

"What did you want to show me?" asked Robbie.

"Nothing," I said.

"But you just told your dad you wanted to show me something."

"I know. I was trying to get him to leave. If we had gone down out of the attic with him, then he would have closed up the stairs. We need them left open for tonight. If we go down now, before he comes back up, I'm hoping he will forget they are open."

"Good thinking," said Robbie.

"Come on!" I said. "I don't want to be in the attic when he comes back. Just be careful. The stairs are really shaky."

We both climbed down and went straight to the bathroom. We brushed our teeth, put on our pajamas, and got into our sleeping bags.

When my mom, my dad, and Suzie came up, we were in my room, looking through the box of baseball cards.

"So, boys, did you find those cards in the guide?" my dad asked.

"Not yet, but we're still looking," I said.

"It's time for bed," said my mom. "You can look some more in the morning."

"Awwww, Mom. Can't we just stay up a few more minutes?"

"Freddy," said my mom, "do you remember what our deal was?"

"Yeah."

"You said that if I let Robbie sleep over, then you would get a good night's sleep. You promised."

Suzie laughed.

"What's so funny?" said my mom.

I gave Suzie the evil eye. She'd better not say anything and ruin our whole plan. "We have a deal," I mouthed at her.

"Oh, nothing," said Suzie. "I was just laughing about something someone told me earlier today."

"When I close this door, I don't want to hear another peep out of you boys," said my mom.

"And no more of that screaming game," said my dad.

"We promise," we said.

"Good night. Sleep tight. Don't let the bed-bugs bite," my parents said.

"Or the monsters," Suzie whispered.

They turned off the light and shut the door.

Now we just had to wait for all of them to go to sleep.

CHAPTER 7

Monster Hunting

Robbie and I told each other ghost stories until the house got quiet.

"Shhhhh," I said. "Listen. I think they have all gone to sleep."

I tiptoed across the floor, opened my bedroom door, and looked out.

I shut the door and tiptoed back over to Robbie. "The coast is clear."

"Then it's time for a little monster hunting," Robbie whispered.

"Yeah. Monster hunting," I whispered. I tried to sound brave, but my voice was shaking.

"Are you okay, Freddy?" Robbie asked. "We don't have to do this if you're too scared."

"Me? Too scared? Nah. I'm fine."

"Then let's get ready," said Robbie.

We put on our black outfits, Robbie grabbed his night-vision goggles, I grabbed my sharkhead flashlight, and we each picked up a hockey stick.

"Ready, Freddy?"

"Ready!"

We walked over to the door and opened it very slowly. I took one step into the hall.

"No! Wait!" Robbie said, yanking me back into the room. I fell down on the ground and dropped my stick.

"Are you crazy?" I said. "We are supposed to be super quiet."

"I know. Sorry. It's just that I remembered we don't have the camera," Robbie whispered.

"Good thing you remembered that now," I

said. "I wouldn't have had the picture to show Max."

I grabbed the camera and put it into my pocket, and we tiptoed down the hall to the guest room.

"Good. Our plan worked. My dad forgot all about putting the stairs back up," I said. "Now, remember, whatever you do, do not step on the fourth step."

Robbie nodded.

"I'll shine my flashlight on the stairs, and you can go up first."

"Thanks, Freddy," said Robbie.

Robbie thought I was being nice, but really I was just being a big wimp. I wanted Robbie to go up first in case the monster was at the top of the stairs waiting for us.

I shined my light on the stairs and Robbie climbed up, skipping the fourth step.

"Do you see anything?" I whispered up to him.

"Nope," he said. "Come on up."

I stuck the hockey stick under one arm so I would have one hand free to grab the side of the stairs. I shined my flashlight on the stairs and climbed up. I was shaking all over. I didn't know which was wobbling more, the stairs or my legs.

When I got to the top, I had to stop for a minute because my heart was beating so fast I thought it was going to pop out of my chest.

"Do you hear anything?" I asked Robbie.

"Nope. It's totally quiet up here."

"Too quiet," I said. "It's kind of creepy."

"It's like he's just waiting to jump out and scare us," said Robbie.

"Did you have to say that?" I asked, biting my nails. "I'm already freaked out enough."

"Sorry," said Robbie. "I'm turning on my night-vision goggles. Come on. Follow me."

We started to walk slowly through the attic. I had my hockey stick up in the ready position

in case the monster jumped out at us. "See anything yet?" I whispered.

"Nope," Robbie whispered back.

We took a few more steps, and that was when I saw it.

I froze in my tracks.

"L-l-l-loooook over there," I said, pointing to the back corner of the attic.

"What is it?" asked Robbie.

I grabbed Robbie's shirt so he had to stop walking. "I . . . I . . . I . . . I think it's the monster!"

Robbie froze. "Where?" he whispered.

"O-o-o-over there," I said again. "In the back corner."

"Are you going to take a picture?" said Robbie.

"No," I said. "It's too far away."

"Well, then we have to move closer," said Robbie.

"Are you crazy?" I whispered. "I am not getting any closer to that thing. He will gobble us up!"

"But if we don't get a picture, then Max won't believe you," said Robbie. "We have to get a picture. Besides, I don't think he's moved at all. He must be sleeping. We'll just walk really quietly and take the picture before he even wakes up."

"How do you know he's not going to wake up?" I said.

"Well, I don't know for sure, but the longer we stand here talking, the greater the chance that he *will* wake up. Come on, Freddy."

Robbie started to walk toward the monster. My feet felt like they were stuck to the ground with glue. They wouldn't move. "I don't think I can do this," I whispered to Robbie.

"Yes, you can, Freddy," Robbie said. "Just get your hockey stick ready and start moving."

I silently counted to three, took a deep breath, and started moving slowly toward the monster. Max Sellars would never be able to call me a baby again if I showed him a picture of the real, live monster in my attic.

After we had taken about three steps, I said, "I think we're close enough."

"Not yet," said Robbie. "It's too dark in here. The flash won't work from that far away."

"The flash? I didn't know the flash was going to go off! That's going to wake up the monster!" I said.

"That's a chance we'll have to take," said Robbie. "Don't stop now. We're so close."

"Yeah. Too close," I thought. I was so nervous I thought I was going to throw up.

"Just a few more steps," said Robbie. "Do you have the camera ready?"

I reached deep down in my pocket for the camera and pulled it out. "I've got the camera," I said.

"On the count of three, take the picture," said Robbie. "I'll be ready with my stick."

I swallowed hard. My hand was shaking so much I didn't think I would be able to hold the camera steady.

"One, two, three," said Robbie. "Now!"

I clicked the button on the camera and the flash went off.

Robbie started laughing.

"Shhhhhh!" I said. "You'll wake up the monster."

"That's not a monster," Robbie said, still laughing. "It's just two old beanbag chairs piled on top of each other with some rolls of wrapping paper sticking out from behind them like horns."

I walked closer to the fake monster. Robbie was right. It was just a pile of old junk. "Great!"

I said. "I got a picture of junk from my attic.
That will impress Max Sellars."

"I think we need to change our plan," said
Robbie.

"What do you mean?" I asked.

"I don't think the monster is here right now,"
said Robbie.

"Where would he be?"

"He must have gone out to get something to
eat," Robbie said.

"I don't even want to think about what he eats," I thought. "So what should we do?" I asked Robbie.

"I think we should hide somewhere up here, so he doesn't see us when he gets back. We could just sit down behind those boxes over there and wait. We'd have to sit very, very still and be very, very quiet."

"You're the genius," I said. "I'll follow you."

We walked over to the other corner of the attic and sat down behind a row of boxes. I could just peek out between two of the larger boxes.

"Now we can see him," said Robbie, "but he can't see us."

"You are so smart, Robbie," I said.

"Keep one hand on your stick, and do not make a sound," said Robbie.

We sat so still that all I could hear was Robbie's breathing and the pounding of my heart.

CHAPTER 8

Proof

The next thing I knew, I heard screeching and something flew by my face.

"AAAAAAHHHHHHHHH!" I screamed. "THE MONSTER!"

I jumped up. Robbie jumped up, and we both ran down the attic stairs, screaming, "AAAAAAAAAHHHHHHHHHH!"

Just as we reached the bottom, my parents ran over to us.

"Freddy. Robbie," said my dad. "What were you two doing up there? Are you okay?"

I looked at Robbie. He looked at me. It was no longer dark. Sunlight was pouring through the windows. We must have fallen asleep while we were waiting for the monster.

"Freddy," said my mom, "what is going on?"

"I . . . I . . . I was monster hunting."

"You were doing what?" said my dad.

"We were monster hunting," I said.

"When did you boys climb up there?" asked my mom.

"Last night," I whispered.

"What?" said my mom. "I didn't hear you."

"Last night."

"Didn't you promise me that you were going to get a good night's sleep?" said my mom.

"Yes, Mom. But the only way I was going to get a good night's sleep was if I got rid of the monster, and Robbie and I had a plan."

My mom and dad started laughing. "Oh, Freddy," said my mom. "You have some of the craziest ideas sometimes."

"How many times have I told you that there is no such thing as monsters?" said my dad.

"Well, you're wrong," I said, "because one is up there right now. It just flew by my head."

"Oh, so now it's a *flying* monster," my mom said, still chuckling.

"If you don't believe me, then go see for yourself," I said.

My dad climbed into the attic and looked around. "I don't see anything," he called down.

Just then we heard the screeching again. "Then wh-wh-what do you call that?" I said.

We heard my dad walking around.

"Be careful, Dad," I yelled. "It might eat you up."

He started to laugh again. "Ha, ha, ha. I found your monster," he said.

"You did?" I said.

"Come up here and take a look."

Robbie and I climbed up into the attic and walked over to where my dad was standing. My dad put his finger to his lips. "Shhhhhhh," he said.

"Is that what I think it is?" Robbie whispered.

My dad nodded.

"It's a bat," said Robbie. "Wow! Freddy, you have a bat living in your attic. That is so cool!"

I just stared and stared at it. "So that's what was making all those scratching and screeching sounds at night?"

"Yes," said my dad. "The scratching, the screeching. That was all from him."

"How did he get in here?" I asked.

"Bats can squeeze in through a hole as small as half an inch," said Robbie.

"Well, we're going to have to call someone to get him out of here," said my dad. "But right now, I think we should all get out of the attic. I don't want our little friend here to fly out into the house since the attic door is open. Come on, let's go."

"Wait, Dad," I said. "I just have to do one more thing." I pulled the camera out of my pocket and took a picture of the bat. "I think

I'll call him Squeaky. Good night, Squeaky.
Sweet dreams," I said as I climbed down the
attic steps.

On Monday morning at school, Max ran up to
me and grabbed my arm. "So, Shark Boy, where's
the picture of that monster in your attic? I bet
you don't have one."

I looked Max right in the eye. "As a matter of fact, I have the picture right here," I said, patting my pocket.

"I don't believe you," said Max. "Let me see it."

I slowly reached into my pocket and pulled out the picture. Max's mouth dropped open. "Is that Dracula in his bat form?" he asked. "You have Dracula living in your attic?"

I just nodded.

"And you took that picture?" Max asked.

"Yes, I did," I said, smiling.

Max's eyes grew big. "Wow! You are braver than I thought, Freddy." Then he shook his head and walked away, leaving me standing there smiling with the picture in my hand.

DEAR READER,

I am a kindergarten and first-grade teacher. I used to live in California, and every year, around Halloween time, I would teach my students about bats. The problem was I never got to see a real bat.

Now I live in Vermont, and there are bats that fly right through my backyard. When I teach my students about bats, they often have interesting bat stories to tell me. There are many farms here in Vermont, and one little girl told me that a whole colony of bats was living in her grandfather's barn! She said that there were at least a hundred bats living in there. She even got to see baby bats holding on to their moms.

Many people are afraid of bats, but they are very gentle creatures. They are also important to the environment because they eat insects. If we didn't have bats, we would have way too many pesky bugs on our planet.

Do you have an interesting bat story? Have you ever had a bat living in your attic? I'd love to hear about it. Just write to me at:

Ready, Freddy! Fun Stuff
c/o Scholastic Inc.
P.O. Box 711
New York, NY 10013-0711

I hope you have as much fun reading *Going Batty* as I had writing it.

HAPPY READING!

Abby Klein

Freddy's Fun Pages

FREDDY'S SHARK JOURNAL

"WATER BATS"

Stingrays look like bats in the water.

Stingrays are cousins of sharks. Both have skeletons of cartilage.

Stingrays live in both freshwater and salt water.

Some stingrays stay buried in the sand, and others are very active swimmers.

Many stingrays have a stinger that contains venom.

Stingrays eat worms, clams, shrimp, and plankton.

Some kinds of stingray babies are born alive from their mother, and some hatch from eggs.

BAT QUIZ:
TRUE OR FALSE?

Are you a bat expert?
Take this bat quiz to find out!

1. Most bats eat what?

2. On what continent are most bats found?

3. What can bats do that no
   other mammal can do?

4. What is the largest bat?

5. About how many different
   types of bats are there?

6. Where do most bats live?

*1. Fruit or insects 2. Africa 3. Fly 4. The flying fox
5. About one thousand 6. In barns, caves, or attics*

EGG-CARTON BATS

Would you like to have some bats
hanging around your house?
Just follow these simple directions
to make these creepy critters, and
then hang them up in different
rooms of your house.

YOU WILL NEED:

an egg carton	scissors
black paint	glue
googly eyes	string or
red yarn	rubber bands

DIRECTIONS:

1. Cut three cups off from an egg carton.
(Keep them connected.)

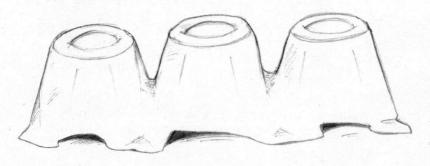

2. Cut the bottoms of the two side cups in a zigzag to make them look like bat wings.

3. Paint the whole thing black.

4. Glue two googly eyes and a small piece of red yarn for the mouth on the middle cup.

5. Attach a string or a rubber band to the top of the middle cup.

Now go batty!

LEARN TO DRAW A BAT

Would you like to learn how to draw a
bat? Just follow these simple steps!

1. Draw an oval
for the body.

2. Draw two upside-down triangles
for the wings. (They should be
touching the body.)

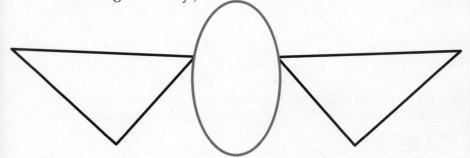

3. Draw two smaller triangles at the top of the oval to make the ears.

4. At the bottom of the oval, draw two straight lines for legs. Add three toes to each leg.

5. Draw two circles near the top of the oval for eyes.

6. Add a mouth (and fangs if you want to).

Have you read all about Freddy?

Don't miss any of Freddy's funny adventures!